Titles available in the
SILVER THIEVES
series
(in reading order)

I0625863

QUEEN'S TREASURE

A CROOK'S TREASURE

SAHARAN TREASURE

TINAN HINAN

Book 3

SAHARAN TREASURE

A.E. STEWART

BUNYA
PUBLISHING.com

SAHARAN TREASURE

ISBN: 978-0-9946151-3-8

*Gary Taaffe
BunyaPublishing.com
BunyaPublishing@gmail.com*

CHAPTER ONE

Tribulations and Congratulations

Africa 1953-1954

J ohn knew that the wonderful news about the baby would impact on his future plans, but he took time to discuss his thoughts about the 'Treasures of Timbuktu' with James.

'I'm so concerned with what is happening to those ancient manuscripts, yet I can't see how I am ever going to be able to help. I knew there was a possibility that we would have a family, but the window of opportunity to rescue those manuscripts is slowly closing.'

'Yes John I see your dilemma but physically there is not much you can do to help. If your language skills included Arabic and other ancient tongues as well as native dialects, you could be of some assistance, but even if you took language courses, time would still be a problem.'

'What makes it worse is the fact that I gave my word to return and assist in any way I could. The hospitality shown to me was much appreciated, and I developed a passionate understanding of what is happening there.'

'Well perhaps you can help in a practical sense if you are willing to consider an Inter-Museum loan to them from us.'

'What a good idea James. The Tuaregs worship Silver, and I am sure that Myra would be agreeable if we sent some of our collection to the Timbuktu Museum. It would be a token of our interest and good faith, as well as keeping our connection with them. It may be possible to set up a scholarship where we could fund some young man to work there in conjunction with our Museum. Of course, he would need the language skills required. I am sure that Myra and I would be happy to donate a greater part of the foundation cost.'

'I think that you might have something there. It sounds like a great idea to help out in a situation which is close to your heart. I feel certain that when this is settled the Museum would be happy to also help with funding.'

This was strongly supported by all who thought that the Silver Exhibition and the Scholarship were excellent ideas. However as time was so important the successful applicant had to be able to currently read or write in some of these other languages. The position was widely advertised in Universities and other Museums, but unfortunately there were not too many wanting to take time off and travel to Timbuktu. When the interviews were held, no more than a dozen applicants applied. The successful applicant had to be able to read and understand some or any of the three main language groups: Afroasiatic, Nilo-Saharan, and Niger-Congo. This whittled down the group of contenders to six men, but when they were told about the ancient Indo-European and Austronesian languages, which were dated from 2,600 and 1000 years ago, the number dwindled down to just one man. His name was Norman Banta, and after graduating from University, he had made Ancient Languages his life's work. He had followed every detail published about this 'Treasure of African History' and had an intense feeling about it. When the scholarship was announced, it was manna from heaven. He wanted to be the chosen one.

Norman was short and middle aged, with a nondescript appearance, but his enthusiasm for this quest made him a compelling force. The candidate had all the necessary qualifications so the Board wasted no time in nominating and accepting Norman. John wrote to the Museum in Timbuktu and also to his colleague Mohammed. He received positive replies from both parties. Their man

Norman Banta, would be made welcome and all courtesies would be extended to him as a revered scholar of such languages as Arabic, Amharic and Hebrew as well as some African dialects.

'There will be some incredible discoveries to be made there. I am sure that you will enjoy that journey. Sadly I cannot accompany you at present.'

'Yes, Mr. Collins I have read accounts of certain French Museums already putting some of the manuscripts on show. I'm aware of the time factor involved here so I will do my best under the tutelage of Timbuktu's Curator.'

A small article in the Cape Town newspaper announced Norman's new post in Mali. Meanwhile Myra and John settled into their cottage and awaited the birth of their first child. The nursery was ready with new furniture, nappies and baby clothes. Myra had been told that it was considered bad luck to do this before the baby arrived, but she dismissed this as an old wives tale. As time went by the household chores became more difficult for her. John asked his wife if she could use some extra help in the house. She agreed. Turning to his friend James Robertson John mentioned this hoping that he could recommend someone to help Myra.

'Yes John, there is such a person who has worked here for many years.

He has often hinted that he would like to change his place of work. I have seen staff come and go but this man has completed any task asked of him with expertise and dignity. He would be an ideal man for the job. Not only would he help Myra inside the house, but he also would be of great assistance outside.'

A surprised look came across John's face.

'You said 'he'. I was expecting you to give me the name of a woman. On your recommendation I will have a talk with him but then you will need to find a replacement.

'Don't worry about that. Jubo has often mentioned his son Dan, who is more than capable to take his father's place. You wouldn't have seen much of Jubo because he works downstairs with the archives, but he is literate, pleasant and intelligent,' affirmed James.

That is how Jubo became part of the Collins family. He fitted perfectly into his new position, loved the freedom of being able to move about outside as well as the variety of the household chores. John had insisted that Jubo live on the property in a small three room flat. He asked Mr. Collins if he could plant a vegetable garden as a source of fresh produce for him to tend when his household chores were done. This was extended to the kitchen where Myra was delighted when he asked her if he could cook some of his own recipes.

She kept her regular appointments with the new local practitioner as her time for giving birth was fast approaching. Jubo spent more time with her in the house and less in the garden, as he showed every care possible. Myra would sometimes catch him looking at her with a worried frown. Then there was the sound of chanting which could be heard coming from his flat at night which seemed a little odd to John who queried this.

'You have been with us for three months now and we both appreciate the tireless effort which you put into every day. Often at night we hear you singing or chanting and I am curious. Is it part of your religion?'

Jubo seemed to be having a slight struggle within before he spoke.

'Mr. Collins I was born in Ethiopia but my family moved to Kenya for various reasons. There was trouble because of tribal unrest, and as I believe the first white settlers gradually took control of this nation, the issue of land ownership became a bitter struggle. My family once again moved south to Cape Town in search of work and a peaceful life. Singing and chanting are part of my heritage. I have always found it comforting when I need to focus on certain issues.'

He continued. 'My parents are dead and my wife died in childbirth delivering a son, who as you know has taken my place at the Museum. Working there in that situation kept me safe.'

'Safe? Is there something that you have to fear? If there is I think that we had better discuss it now. Please go ahead Jubo. It is important that I understand what you are talking about.'

'I am so fortunate to live and work here and I would hate to leave but you deserve to know even if you do not like what I have to say. There is a groundswell of native support for a rebellion in Kenya because of the decades of opposition against the militant years of oppressive colonial rule. Wages paid to the workers were very low but the idea of national independence was too difficult for people who were buried in tribalism. Unfortunately there is an uprising in Nairobi because of the curfews imposed and there are gangs of arsonists who have been punishing Africans who refuse to join their Mau Mau rebellion.'

'I hear what you are saying, as I feel the unfolding of a serious situation, but I am pleased that we have had this discussion because the years that I have lived in Africa have opened my eyes to what I call 'anti-colonial politics.' I am very much aware of the inequities which exist all over this great country. Even here in South Africa the Apartheid is a rooted evil which needs exorcising but Jubo please explain why you need to feel safe?'

'I did not agree with the line taken by some of my friends and showed my lack of support by moving out. They would possibly think that I ran away, and

11

would not have appreciated my opinion about the situation.'

'Thank you for your honesty Jubo. Perhaps we will discuss this further some other time.'

Jubo returned to his vegetable garden with a heavy heart, because this conversation had revived terrible memories which had been hidden for years. He had only just managed to escape with his life so he knew that he couldn't afford to be complacent about his safety if his enemies should seek him. Pushing these thoughts to the back of his mind, he set off for the market. Tonight he intended to cook a special meal.

Myra was intrigued.

'I have never tasted anything like it. Please tell me more about it.'

Jubo's smile was wide enough to show his missing tooth but he was happy to receive her praise and to explain all about it.

'This is a national dish from Ethiopia and is called 'Injera'. Usually this pancake bread is so large that it overlaps the serving tray. The diner breaks off portions before filling them with assorted meats as I have served to you. Cottage cheese and yoghurt are always served as the stews can be a lot spicier than what I have made tonight. This is because I am concerned that the baby might not like it.'

Jubo need not have worried. It was a meal that was much appreciated by both John and Myra. When

Myra visited her local doctor she was given some disturbing news. The fetus was in "breech presentation." Although the doctor earlier suspected this, he also knew that twenty five per cent of fetuses were in the breech position at thirty two weeks gestation, but this figure drops to three per cent at term. Because of possible complications, an umbilical cord prolapse could occur and diminish the oxygen flow to the baby. It is possible to 'turn' the baby to avoid breech birth, but this must be done by a competent midwife or doctor. The other option is to have a Caesarean section.

John suggested they get another opinion from an Obstetrician before making any decision. Myra was visibly upset.

'I was hoping for a natural and uncomplicated birth. I never dreamed I would have to face these problems.'

The meeting with an Obstetrician confirmed that the baby was indeed in breech position, but he assured them that he was skilled and knowledgeable with all variations of this type of case.

'There are a couple of important things to consider. These are: if you opt for a Caesarean, it has a lower risk to the fetus but a slightly increased risk to the mother than a planned vaginal delivery. If this is scheduled in advance, before the onset of labour it could be also a risk of delivering the baby too early with possible complications of prematurity. The other option is the external cephalic version, where the baby is turned by manipulations through the mother's abdomen. When this is done, the baby's heart is monitored, usually without any complications on the presentation at term. You have some decisions to make, so please discuss it before you let me know.'

'Sleep on it tonight my darling, and tomorrow we can make a clear decision,' said John as he gently helped her to bed. Before he turned off the light he could hear that soft chanting coming through the window from Jubo's flat. At breakfast they sat down to a platter of fresh fruits including bananas, grapes, figs, chunks of orange and yoghurt, when they discussed their impending choice which had to be made with the safety of both Mother and baby. There wasn't much of a choice as Myra saw it. If the Obstetrician could move the baby into the correct position for a normal birth, then that had to be the best way. John rang and arranged for his wife to be at the hospital in two days. In the meantime she should take a gentle walk around the garden.

John decided to tackle Jubo about his chanting.

'Mr.Collins, I have been singing to the evil spirits and asking them not to harm the baby because I can sense that all is not going to plan. In Ethiopia it was not considered wise to prepare and furnish a room before the baby arrived safely into the world. This was thought to draw attention to dark spirits which could mark the child for disaster. I have seen the nursery and I felt worried about that, but now I have heard that Mrs. Collins has some other issues too so I shall pray and sing with more focus.'

'If you think that this will help, I shall not interfere except to ask you to do it quietly with the doors and windows closed, but I feel sure that our specialist has this problem under complete control.'

Myra did feel a little pressure when the baby was gently manipulated externally, but there was no pain or discomfort. The monitor said that all was normal so she was allowed home after a few hours to await the arrival of their baby. They both agreed that John should go to work for at least a half day. Jubo had the telephone number for the ambulance as well as the hospital so Myra was happy for her husband to be occupied with his work.

She was sitting on the verandah enjoying a cool lemon squash with some home made cookies. A gentle breeze stirred the air, leaving Myra totally relaxed. She asked Jubo to sit with her for a while.

'I believe that you originally came from Ethiopia. Tell me what it was like there?'

'Yes I was born and educated there, but my family migrated back and forth between settler farms constantly looking for work. My mother insisted that I learn to read and write, teaching me when she could. We eventually came to Nairobi in Kenya but there were serious indications of violent unrest which resulted in the deaths of both my parents. The impact of colonial rule has been an ongoing problem since 1895, and I fear that it is not over yet.'

Myra didn't want to discuss politics, so she changed the subject.

She realized that Jubo's high cheekbones and fine features were direct evidence of his forebears, so she decided to talk about her Ethiopian bracelets.

'Soon enough I will become a new Mum and perhaps a very busy one even with your help, but there is something which I want to show you before all that takes place. If you were educated by your Mother, I assume that you can read the symbols and words of your language. Is that correct?'

'Yes, Mrs. Collins.'

'Good, I have here with me a small diary and on this page you will see a large circle with a strange outline and also some engraved symbols. Have you ever seen anything like this before?'

He studied it for a while but was completely at a loss as to what it meant. Something stirred in his brain which reminded him of an old story told by his Mother, but the details were lost.

'No, some of the symbols are similar to Ethiopian letters but without any visible pattern which I can follow. The raised outline looks a little like a view of a city with its rooftops, but I'm sorry to say that is all I can tell you. When I worked in the Museum I often spent my spare time reading and researching the history of Ethiopia. I think that perhaps you might find something there to help you identify this circle.'

When John arrived home he was pleased to hear that his wife and Jubo had been chatting about Ethiopia, but when she told him about Jubo's suggestion to research her drawing from the Museum's books, John strongly disagreed.

'Myra my dearest, it will be some time before you can do anything like that. Perhaps for the time being it would be better if I bring some home and we can both bury our noses in them.'

'O.K. that sounds fine. I'm off to bed early tonight.'

She bent over to kiss her husband goodnight and felt the baby give a solid kick. It shouldn't be long now, she thought to herself.'

John sat up for a while reading the newspapers which carried alarming news. In British East Africa, (later known as Kenya), a civil war was turning into a military offensive between a Kikuyu dominated anti-colonial group called the Mau Mau and the elements of the British Army, auxiliaries and anti-Mau Mau Kikuyu. The fact that various tribes were not united meant that they were no match for the European settlers and the reserves which were set up to contain different ethnic groups, became overcrowded with little recourse to improve the living conditions. A serious problem was the fact that there were members of the Kikuyu fighting against the Mau Mau on the side of the colonial government, but there were also many other Kikuyu involved with the Mau Mau and the violent rebellion. This whole episode was like a creeping epidemic and John was not sure that he was immune to its import.

The next morning Myra was up early to take her usual walk around the garden but after a few steps she felt a strange sensation. Realising that her waters had broken she found a bench seat beneath a tree and called to Jubo.

'Is the baby coming?' he asked.

Myra took a deep breath. 'Yes Jubo, please ring for the ambulance and then my husband. I will be okay here whilst you do this.'

He ran inside, made both calls but when he returned to the spot where he left her, she was nowhere to be seen. Jubo called out loudly but no answer came. Then he ran back into the house looking in every room. Where was she? Once again he made a quick trip around the garden, calling to her and trying to keep the panic out of his voice. Something was terribly wrong.

Jubo had felt uneasy about the coming birth when he first took employment here. The fear when his wife had died giving birth came back clearly to him. The same helplessness washed over him. Looking for some sign of her, his eyes slowly swept around the fence line of the property. He had looked everywhere except in his own little flat. Could she have gone there? It seemed unlikely, and anyway she would have heard him calling out to her.

Jubo ran towards it, but as he did he noticed two narrow lines dug into the damp grass leading to his front door. If she was in there she had been dragged there against her will. Ducking his head beneath the window his heart was hammering as he ran around to the back door which was never locked. Quietly opening the door, Jubo knew that the kitchen would provide him with some sort of a weapon Passing through the passageway he picked up a sharp knife from the chopping block and quickly hid it inside his shirt.

The scene before him left him unprepared. Mrs. Collins was tied to his bed with a length of thick rope and a man whom he recognised, was bending over her with a knife to her throat. Myra's eyes widened with fear, but her mouth was gagged so she could only groan. Looking at her he knew that she was possibly in labour, and he had better think twice about every step before taking it. He waited for his old enemy to speak.

'Ah, Jubo you have fallen into a very comfortable position in this household, but this woman is in big trouble. I did not come here to harm her but I will if you don't listen and obey my every word. For some years I have been searching for you but until last week I had no success. You were seen at the market place by one of my men who followed you home.

Today I waited until her husband left, and as you can see, she is in no condition to give any trouble so I can finish the job that I came here to do. You never should have deserted our cause where you could have been such a leader of men, but to make it worse you took my sister away with you. I know that she died giving you a son, but as he is of my blood too he will remain safe. That is not the same fate that I have in mind for you.'

Jubo knew how important it was to keep Maloba talking as it would give the ambulance time to arrive.

'Maloba, you were like a brother to me. We both witnessed floggings and the unjust treatment of our people, but I could never understand why you were involved with the killings and atrocities made in the name of a rebellion against our own countrymen. I could not stop it, because there were so many divided both for and against the Mau Mau, but I chose to take my wife and our unborn child to a safer place away from all the horror.'

Maloba smiled mirthlessly. He knew that Jubo worked for a wealthy man and that there must be cash or valuables in the house which he could put to good use. After listening to this conversation of controlled hate from Maloba, Myra knew that Jubo's calm and honest appeal for understanding had evaporated into the air. She felt a little flutter within her and hoped that the baby was not taking this very inconvenient time to enter into the world. All her hopes rested with Jubo and his handling of this terrible situation. Still Jubo tried to reason with him.

'I cannot expect you to understand my way of thinking but your sister totally agreed with my decision to flee from the lands of death and deprivation. For a short time we were content here. Despite living with 'Apartheid,' I earned enough to support us. More importantly we were not fighting brother against brother in a civil war.'

Maloba lost his patience and roared at Jubo.

'Enough of this stupidity! Let's get on with it. I will take anything of value which can be used to support our cause. Don't try anything clever, as you know how well I can use this knife.' As they left Myra allowed herself a small whimper as the flutters began to come at regular intervals. Surely the ambulance must be close by, and where was John?

Jubo walked ahead of Maloba very slowly but his mind was racing. He couldn't take any risks which would jeopardise the arrival of the coming baby, but he knew that his life also hung on a slender thread. For now he had to agree to everything asked of him until the right moment to seize his only chance. Inside the house he showed Maloba the collection of Antique Silver within a locked cabinet. After producing the key he stood back whilst they were inspected.

'Are these what you are looking for? The cash box is in the drawer below. You will need a large bag to hold all these items. There is one in the laundry.'

Maloba was cunning and he suspected that perhaps Jubo would try something so he said to him.

'I will come with you to get the bag.' Knowing that the fate of Mrs. Collins and her unborn child did not bear thinking about, Jubo also knew that Maloba would not hesitate in inflicting an unspeakable death on this innocent woman. He saw his chance and took it. Picking up a burlap sack of potatoes he calmly emptied them into the sink. Then he wrapped the bag around his arm and reached for the knife hidden beneath his shirt simultaneously. For a moment Maloba was caught off guard but years of training had not deserted him. His hate made him an automatic opponent as he raised his knife at Jubo. With the element of surprise Jubo was quicker, sinking his weapon into Maloba's throat. The Hessian bag caught Maloba's downward thrust, but it was deflected and there was little damage done to Jubo. Maloba desperately tried to use his knife again but his jugular vein had been severed.

A look of disbelief lasted for two seconds before he slumped to the floor like air escaping from a balloon, as his blood spurted out in a crimson arc with gurgling sounds rushing from his drowning throat. As soon as Jubo confirmed that his attacker was dead, he raced across the lawn to his little home where he found Myra in a state of distress. Quickly he removed her gag and the confining rope. She started to pant and he knew that the pains were coming frequently and stronger. The baby must be on its way. Myra looked wildly up at Jubo. When she could concentrate on something beside the terrible wracking pain, she grunted.

'This baby is nearly here and you will have to help me deliver it. Put some water on to boil in the kitchen and then hold me whilst I push down.'

He did as he was told but Myra's scream brought him back into reality. For a moment he had been back with his own wife when she gave birth. This time would be different. He would not let Myra down. Holding her as strongly as he could whilst she was thrashing around and yelling, Jubo forgot all about the Ambulance as he willed this baby to arrive safely. At last after one long piercing cry Myra delivered the baby. The umbilical cord had to be cut but he had used his sharpest knife on Maloba, so he went looking for another in his kitchen. Just as he did this the door of his modest home flew open and in rushed John followed by the two ambulance men. Despite the fact that Jubo had a small knife in his hand, John knew exactly what had happened.

The men took over the necessary task of cutting the cord and wrapping the baby before placing it on Myra's breast. John was lost for words as he gently kissed Myra's face. She smiled and said.

'I may be exhausted but will someone please tell me whether we have a boy or a girl?'

Jubo proudly answered 'We have a boy.'

Mother and child were taken to hospital for observation. John promised to follow as soon as he had cleared up a few things in the house. Despite Jubo's connection with the dead man, he owed the life of his wife and son to him. There was no need to divulge all the details to the police. It was reported and accepted as a home invasion by an unknown intruder. Any reference to the Mau Mau may have ramifications which would not serve any purpose.

In a short time Mother and son returned home. From all indications they both were doing well. Seated in the lounge-room, Myra presented the baby to Jubo and told him that they had decided to name their son: James, Jubo, David, Collins. He was delighted.

'Mr. and Mrs. Collins, you have done me a great honour by giving my name to your son. Accepting my innocence in this awful catastrophe without any criticism is also very much appreciated. You will always be a part of my family and I shall protect your little son in any way that I can.'

'After what we have all just been through, I think that we can dispense with some of the formalities. In future please call us by our Christian names.' Myra said.

TRIBULATIONS AND CONGRATULATIONS

'Yes we owe you so much and will always consider you as our friend and invaluable employee,' agreed John.

Jubo knew that his employers could have taken a very different approach to the fact that he had made a dangerous enemy who had brought danger and possible death into their lives.

'By the way, when you have some spare time I think that we could add another room to your flat.'

Jubo was speechless as the emotion rose in his throat. He just nodded, gave a large toothy grin and moved back into the kitchen.

Myra decided to phone her sister and give her the good news about the safe arrival of James Collins. Jill was happy to hear from Myra hinting that perhaps next year when James was a little older, they might take a trip to visit them. She spoke a little about her husband Brian and the two children (who were an interesting age now), and how much they wanted to meet their new cousin.

The latest news from Australia was about an incident when the Russian KGB came to deport two Embassy officials back to Russia. All the newspapers carried the story about Vladimir and Evdokia Petrov, with a photo of her being escorted to the waiting plane with one shoe missing. Her husband had decided to defect but his wife was not too sure about her decision. Eventually she decided to do the same, but not before the whole affair had turned into an ugly situation. Myra did not comment too much about this, because the political news in South Africa was not filled with any joy. For some years there was a growing resistance to the Apartheid policies of the government. A man called Nelson Mandela was supporting this opposition. Although she didn't discuss politics with her husband, she had heard him talking with Jubo, and his attitude did not condone this 'apartness,' as he called it.

A letter was sent to Ikey with all the details about James, Jubo, David Collins. He was so pleased to get the good news, replying with a letter which included a crisp five pound note: a gift for the baby.

'I did get a bit of a shock when I read your letter because at first I thought you had delivered triplets. Then my wife, ('er indoors) explained that your son had three names. A little bit different I told her, but she said Royalty always does it, so why not you?

Archibald (as Archie likes to be called) is courting a nice young woman and they both have similar interests in the Antique Silver market. Her name is Amanda and they met at College where he has been learning all kinds of things including how to talk propper. The missus and I will probably be retiring in a few years and moving down to Brighton to be near her sister (ugh), to enjoy the climate and the scenery, if you get my meaning. When that happens perhaps Archibald will be ready to take over the business. Who knows?

TRIBULATIONS AND CONGRATULATIONS

Merv is happier than a mudlark, and he is now one very contented cove. Always singing and whistling as that coffee shop and Flo keep him occupied and busy. Sometimes he comes over for a chat but I have to shut him up. He babbles on constantly and almost gives me a headache. I think that I could go outside make a pot of tea, come back and he would still be going on about something. Marriage has certainly given him a new spark of life.

Speaking about wives, mine wished to be remembered to you both and told me to say that she is eagerly waiting for photos of the baby. Please give him a kiss from us. To you and yours I say Shalom until the next time.

Your friend, Ikey Solomon.'

— CHAPTER TWO —

The Silver Stage

Africa and England 1954

Myra was kept busy looking after their baby, but Jubo insisted that he take on the role of nursemaid as well as his other duties. It seemed that a bond was forged on the day that James was born. Jubo hated to be away from his charge for any long period of time. After three months Myra weaned her baby and Jubo was more than happy to bottle feed this little man. Jubo got his extra room and a verandah, but spent less time in it as most of his day was spent with James in the house.

Ikey received a letter with the promised photos of James and his parents and also one with Jubo cradling the baby in his arms. It all looked so different to the life which they had shared in London. Even the bungalow set in a large garden with brilliant flowering trees completed the picture of a happy suntanned couple with their first child; so different to London's cold and drab scenery.

'Dear Myra and John,' wrote Ikey.

'Thank you for those lovely photos. My missus was right proud to see you all looking so well and happy. We would love to see the baby one day. No matter, please send us photos as he grows when you can. Now to another matter.

As you know Archibald has become quite interested and knowledgeable in the Antique Silver business. You would remember that night when we helped you pack and invoice the objects found beneath the stairs how Archie had a good memory and an eye for quality. Recently he was informed of an auction which was featuring 'Flatware,' and he became very interested. He managed to hide his enthusiasm but when he viewed these articles his curiosity turned to animosity. He feels sure that these pieces are the missing ones which never reached you when the others were shipped out. The only way that he could identify them would be if he had a copy of the inventory with the identifying hallmarks, but as there is not time for that before the auction, he is stymied. He is willing to bid for them just to identify the vendor, but this would be a long shot and also hard to prove that they have been stolen. How do you feel about this?

By the way, my wife gets a piece of Wedgwood for every Birthday, Anniversary and Christmas and she doesn't complain about feeling poorly so much anymore. Funny the power of pottery, eh?

We all send our very best wishes to you. Kind regards from Ikey.'

John decided to immediately phone Ikey with his thoughts about the letter.

'Hello Ikey. Thanks for the news about Archibald and the possible missing Silver but I am afraid that time is against us as far as the Auction is concerned. It would take too long for me to send photographic proof of the inventory. If Archie suspects that these are our silverware pieces, I would put every faith in his judgment. The co-incidence seems too much to be ignored but the long arm of the law cannot stretch from here to London. If he can somehow trace the pieces back to the seller perhaps something can be done then?'

'I hear what you are saying John, but this sounds as if it is a little too much for him to handle alone. Even his lady friend Amanda has serious reservations about the whole caper.'

'Ah that makes things a little different. Is it possible for both of them to attend the Auction and bid against each other?'

'Well yes I expect so but what good would that do?'

'Ikey my friend we can bait the hook with two worms and make the odds swing a little more in our favour. If they can afford to outlay a good sum for only one of these pieces, they will be in a good position to have the evidence in their hands as well as the details of the person who put them up for sale. I trust that Amanda is a young attractive woman who can make her presence felt at such occasions?'

'She is that and more. I don't know what she sees in Arch, but that's another story. Not only is she intelligent but she is what I would call a knockout.'

'Good Ikey if she is prepared to help out she could be the key to the whole thing. A beautiful young woman could be a useful distraction. Without putting too fine a point on it, I seem to remember that you knew a few characters or fences, that could also be of help. Discuss this with Archibald and Amanda. I am sure that they will know just how to handle it. In the meantime I will have the inventory copied and sent express post to you. Let me know how this turns out. Goodbye for now.'

James was now six months old, beginning to show his own personality, with definite likes and dislikes. He would go into fits of giggles whenever Jubo would sing or dance, and wasn't the least bit worried if Mum and Dad were too busy elsewhere to cater to his needs. This was a mutual love affair as far as Jubo was concerned as he doted on the child and would often take James in his stroller around the garden, talking to him in his own language and pointing out the birds and insects with an imitation of their songs. Of course James had no cognition of these words, but because of this early introduction to another language, James grew to understand and later recognise African dialects and expression.

This was a few years away but Jubo planted the first seeds of language familiarity in the life of this little child. His position in this household was strong and welcomed by his employers. His cuisine and customs were initiated from his birthplace but they were accepted into this family with great appreciation. This included the washing and wiping of hands at the table before the meal was served.

John suggested that Jubo might like to invite his son to join them for dinner when they all could enjoy Jubo's Ethiopian cuisine. The invitation was accepted with pleasure by Dan who arrived after work from the Museum. He had heard a lot about the family, and was happy to meet them under such pleasant circumstances to share a meal.

Myra was surprised to hear that Dan had a European name. Jubo was quick to explain.

'Dan is named after our ancestors from the tribe of Dan which were Ethiopian Jews. These trans-migrants established communities in many places such as Gao and Timbuktu. The proof of these old Jewish communities can be found in the notable archives which I have been told exist in Timbuktu. We don't practice the Jewish religion, because over the centuries the whole of Africa north of the Sahara desert was conquered by the armies of Islam. Trade dictated that conversions were made mainly for that purpose but although in some opinions this had little to do with faith, Islam took root and grew.'

John was fascinated with this account and asked Jubo what he knew about the legend of the Queen of Sheba and King Solomon.

'We don't believe that this was a legend. Menelik was the son of King Solomon and Queen Sheba or Makeda as we call her. Both these royal persons are referenced within the Christian, Hebrew and Koran biblical accounts, so it cannot be considered in any way that they were part of a legend. According to Ethiopian tradition, many believe that Haile Selassie I, born Tafari Makonnen to be of direct blood lineage from Menelik 1. This has been a fact of debate among African scholars but there is no denial that Royal imperial families continue on the African continent.'

After the amber coloured wine and sweet black coffee were served, Dan was asked to perform the hand washing custom. He smiled at this symbolic request because he knew that this couple was highly esteemed by his Father. He left that night having enjoyed being part of a family tradition which appreciated his culture as well as his company.

Once Myra heard the story about Solomon and Sheba from Jubo, she wanted to know more about them. James was crawling and possibly cutting his first tooth, so he was put into a play pen where he happily sucked and chewed on his soft rag toys. His

Mum was wrapped in concentration listening to Jubo.

'The Queen of Sheba or Makeda is referred to in the Bible books of Kings and Chronicles as well as the New Testament, the Qur'an and Ethiopian history books. Her kingdom is still the subject of speculation, but it is considered to be either in Yemen or Eritrea, Ethiopia. King Solomon was very interested in trade, engaging the services of a merchant from Sheba's kingdom to help transport certain valuables for him. At this time Egypt was all powerful with Ethiopia a close second in power and fame, but the merchant was impressed with the magnificent buildings which he saw in Israel. On his return to Ethiopia he described the culture of the Jewish people and how the compassion and wisdom of its King had overawed him.

When Sheba heard this she decided to make a journey. This was no ordinary journey because she came with many camels carrying gold, precious stones and spices of great magnitude.

Black women of antiquity were known for their love affairs as well as their beauty. To say that she made a great impact on Solomon and his people is to gravely underestimate her. Every need was fulfilled including an apartment specially built for her stay in Jerusalem. As Solomon traveled about his kingdom Sheba accompanied him, observing his judgment and prudence which greatly impressed her. Although

Solomon had a harem with wives and concubines he was smitten with her and took her as his lover. When she eventually left Israel he placed a ring on her finger and said.

"If you have a son, give this to him and send him to me." Sheba did have a son. When he became an adult she sent him to Solomon who accepted him as his first born son, but Menelik decided to return to his homeland where he ruled wisely and well. Today the ruler of Ethiopia is known as the "Conquering Lion of Judah", descended directly from King Solomon and Queen Sheba.'

Myra was enthralled by this powerful story told by Jubo. She appreciated his account of something which was part of his own heritage. This country which was now her homeland had a wonderful rich history. She was learning how little she knew about it.

John was true to his word and had a photocopy made of the inventory to send 'Express Post,' to Ikey. Unfortunately they had not been photographed but he remembered each one, accurately describing them together with the hallmark details which he had with the original inventory. After a short space of time a letter arrived from Ikey. By the sound of his elation in the first few lines all had gone to plan.

'My boy Archibald was wonderful. Both he and Amanda had a meeting with some of my old fences (I mean colleagues). They worked out a scam that was unbelievable. It has all been sorted. It went something like this. When I told them about your idea, they was a little skeptical. But to give her credit, Amanda had the germ of an idea when I mentioned that I could also find some other helpers to attend the Auction and throw a spanner in the works, you might say.

A meeting was held at my place where I spoke to them about your suggestion to confuse and upset the whole procedure. Amanda and Archie considered that they had to keep a respectable profile in case they attended other similar auctions, so it was up to the others to help with the set-up. Both Amanda and Arch went as themselves as separate bidders, but the other four men and one lady (an ex-actress called Kitty) dressed up a treat. This lady was regaled in all the fake costume jewelry and a massive fur coat that her body could support. No one could miss her with that heavily made up face, and her role was to interrupt the proceedings by harassing Amanda. The other four men were dressed in various styles of clothing which suggested other professions. They sat at random positions around the room. Once the auction commenced Archie and Amanda made their bids against each other but so did a few other interested parties who soon dropped off as the bids became higher. Two objects were secured at a much dearer price than they were worth but the success of this intention was achieved. At a pre-arranged signal Amanda began to loudly cough. This is when the actress went into action. She yelled and waved her fist at Amanda and moved towards her with a menacing intent, as two of the planted men tried to hold her back. She was having none of it and kept calling Amanda dreadful names and screaming bodily threats. The two men trying to protect Amanda had to deal with a lot of pushing and shoving as the other patrons decided to leave.

Someone took a swing at a bystander (which didn't land) and another enraged man began verbally abusing Kitty. This only inflamed the situation and before long, a real donnybrook took place. Chairs were overturned as a couple fell over each other. The attendant took one look at this scene and decided that he was not the fighting type and quickly disappeared. When he could be heard above this terrible din, the auctioneer tried to unsuccessfully bring the place to order, but by that time it was too late. Archibald stepped up to the auctioneer and informed him that he was interested in buying the whole collection as a separate sale from the vendor. Showing obvious relief that all was not lost the Auctioneer listened to Archie's request with consent. He had noticed that Archie was comforting the beautiful young woman who was a victim of some unprovoked attack by an ugly harridan, who had mistaken her for someone else. She was wiping her eyes with a lace handkerchief and looked so shaken that he felt a real sympathy for her.

When Archie explained that both he and this young lady were prevented from acquiring anything more due to the commotion, he assured the Auctioneer that they were still keen to buy anyway. This seemed a reasonable request so he rung the vendor and explained about the awful disruption but thankfully he had a couple of buyers who were still interested in the collection. The seller agreed and gave the address which turned out to be a warehouse in a shabby part of London. Archie drove to this place while the four 'colleagues' waited outside in a furniture van just in case.

Inside the seller seemed a little nervous at first, but Amanda played her part very well, picking up and putting down pieces, talking to herself and generally wasting time. This was done so that Archie could get his bearings and make sure that they were alone. Eventually she chose two items: the Asparagus tongs and the Moustache spoon.

When Archie asked the price for the remaining collection he was surprised how little the man wanted. He obviously didn't know their real value. He agreed, informing the cove that he would have to go to the bank for the cash, but would return in about an hour. So as to not raise any suspicion Amanda paid for her two pieces then turned to leave. This put the seller's mind at rest. He was not prepared for the four heavies who came in the door and quickly overpowered him. They bundled him into the van before a quick trip to the cop shop.

As they say, the rest is history. This criminal was well known to the police so they gladly took him into custody. The evidence was also presented with the exception of eight pieces which must have 'somehow fallen off the back of the van' as they say. Archibald had a word with arresting officer and told him that these pieces belonged to a colleague of his who was sending the proof of ownership by mail from South Africa. So you see my friends, after the long winded description of the debacle which returned most of your lost goods, you have now a positive outcome.

If I can suggest this, it possibly would be better to leave these items here where Archie can sell them for you. I have a few out of pocket expenses for the actress who deserves some recompense for the wonderful part played she played in all of this.

(I had the devil's own job trying to convince my missus that Kitty and me were not more than friends). Justice has been done and we are happy with the result. I hope that you both agree.

Once again we send our very best to you and baby James.

Your friend and colleague, Ikey.'

— CHAPTER THREE —

Dan's Discovery

Africa and England 1954

After reading this letter John and Myra were amazed at the results this group had accomplished. Not only had Archie and Amanda kept their reputation intact, but the flatware had been recovered almost in its entirety. John asked Myra if she would agree to forfeit the funds received when the silver was sold. She turned to him and said.

'I know you well enough to know that something is being hatched in your brain. What are you thinking about?'

'Well my love, I would like to think that when we get it, we can put the money realised on the sale of the flatware into better use than leave it sitting in the bank.'

'Whatever do you mean by 'forfeit'? She said.

'If we can arrange it legally I would like to help Archie buy out Ikey's business as we both know that he wants to retire. Our Solicitor could hold this money for us until that happens. Archie could then access it and use it as a deposit when needed. He could pay it back over a protracted time into an account set up for us in England.

I am thinking about an investment in the future education of our son in the long term, as well as giving Archie the chance to buy Ikey's shop in the short term.'

When she heard this, Myra threw back her head and laughed.

'John you are forgetting that James isn't even a year old yet. Already you are thinking about his teenage years. What about the good schools in this country?'

'No, I am not forgetting his age but I know that some of the best English schools have a waiting list for five or ten years. If we put our son's name down now we may be lucky enough to enroll him for his senior years.'

'After all we have been through just to have a healthy child I can't agree to your ideas about his future education, but I have no objection to helping out Archie in this way. Perhaps in a few years we can all travel to England and visit our friends too.'

John wrote to Ikey and instructed him to pay Kitty whatever he thought was reasonable and to deduct that payment from the proceeds of the flatware. He also wrote to their Solicitor telling him of his plan to assist Archibald if he was interested in purchasing Ikey's business. This would be discussed at length, so he didn't expect a reply.

That week Dan celebrated his birthday. Jubo asked if he could invite him to dine with them. This was welcomed by Myra and John as they knew that Jubo would produce something very special. He didn't disappoint them. James was allowed to sit in his high chair but after he ate, he became fidgety and kept reaching out for Jubo who was trying to serve the meal. Myra decided that it was time for James to go to bed so they could eat in peace. When the meal and the washing of hands were finished Myra followed Dan into the kitchen where he started to do the dishes.

'It is your birthday Dan you shouldn't be doing this. I'll wash them but I would like to hear all about your job at the Museum.'

Up until now Dan had been fairly quiet, only replying when he was asked a question.

'I have a wonderful opportunity to learn and discover so many facts about Ethiopia and Africa. I work undisturbed downstairs in the bowels of the Museum but there are so many wonders stored there, that just the books and artifacts keep me engrossed. The time passes so quickly that I almost regret when it is closing time. If I sound a little boring it is because I have never had such knowledge at my fingertips, and there is so much more to read and discover.

When I knew that your husband had opened a scholarship to visit the Manuscripts of Timbuktu, I was so disappointed because I didn't have the knowledge of those ancient languages. Since then I have started to study some of them when I have the time.'

'That sounds wonderful Dan keep it up. Who knows? In a year or two you could join Norman Banta as his assistant. I know that Mr.Collins has a great passion for the rescue of these ancient books. Do you have any knowledge of the Ethiopian written language?'

'Yes I have a little because I have been reading it since I began working to re-acquaint myself with our past. I have been told that there is still much to learn about Ethiopia at Timbuktu.'

Myra hesitated for a moment, but she felt that if she didn't take this opportunity now, she might never do it.

'If I show you an etching that I made in Timbuktu which was identified as possibly being made in Ethiopia do you think that you could tell me something about it?'

'I will try Mrs. Collins,' Dan said.

As he studied her etchings, Dan felt that he had seen something like this during his research. He felt that the etching depicted a skyline of some city and was possibly a kind of map with hidden but confusing details.

'If you notice how the extremities have what could be towers and bridges as well as pointed roofs in a random pattern, this could identify a certain place. As to the engraved symbols, I cannot decipher them at all. There is a city called Marib in Yemen which according to what I have read, was the capital of the Sabaean Kingdom or as the Hebrews knew it: Sheba. This city is now sadly barren, dry and in ruins, but once it was a lush oasis with plants and trees and was ideally situated on the trade routes. The ruins have been scattered but what I have seen in this drawing remind me of what was only an artist's impression of the old city skyline.

The other site could be Abalessa which was a kingdom in the Ahaggar Mountains in Algeria, which was sometimes known as Skyscraper City. A much loved Queen called Tin Hanan was a famous monarch who was known as 'Mother of us all.' Neither of these two places are in Ethiopia, but if you want me to take the book I will do some research on your drawings.'

'Thank you Dan you have given me something to think about, and I will also do a little research myself. Perhaps then we can compare our findings. In the meantime, good luck with your studies.'

Dan thanked them then said goodnight. Myra was a little despondent because both of the cities described by Dan were so far away. She had little hope of visiting them. When she told John about this discussion she became even more confused when he bought home a book with illustrations of the 'Great Mosque of Djenne' at Mali. Not only was this building known as the Largest Mud Brick Building on Earth with an abundant Islamic influence, (said to have been built in the 13th century), but it also featured the strange similar roof pattern.

'We were there,' Myra said to her husband. 'We went to Timbuktu for our honeymoon. Why didn't I notice that roof pattern?'

'There was no reason or time to explore that place. I was looking at old manuscripts which completely dominated my mind. Until you wanted those two bracelets we had no links to any skylines of buildings.'

'I will dismiss the Mosque idea because you were told by Mohammed's friend that the bracelet was Ethiopian and not from this area. Wasn't that right?'

'Yes, he told us that it was a Bedouin design and although not unlike the Tuareg patterns he felt that it originated from Ethiopia.'

'If that was true, why was he involved in my rescue? I would have thought that the bracelets were important to him or to the men who took me, only if the bracelets were made locally. In other words, what earthly use would they be to him or those men if they were made in Ethiopia?'

'Mm, you may have a point there. I will take this query to my old friend James at the Museum and see what he has to say. There is no point in jumping to conclusions until we make some systematic investigation and find some facts to help identify them.'

When John discussed this with James he omitted nothing about the two bracelets and their possible origins.

'So my friend, am I correct in thinking that your clever little wife made an etching from both of these bracelets before they were exchanged for her freedom? If so they were obviously very important to someone. Otherwise they wouldn't have made such a bungled attempt to steal them. I would like to have a closer look at these etchings.'

When John rang Myra to tell her about James's comments, she didn't hesitate and immediately invited him home for dinner. James enjoyed the meal and their company but was keen to get down to the purpose of his visit. John placed a dark cloth beneath the paper impressions so that they were easier to read. James studied them closely, using a magnifying glass before he said.

'Starting at the beginning I will call these bracelets and not bangles because as you can see, they have a locking device which was used to open them easily. Unlike bangles which can only fit over a wrist, these two could have been worn on the wrist or around the ankles.'

'What do you mean? Are these slave bracelets?' asked Myra.

'No not necessarily so, because with all these patterns which spike away from the central circle, they could be quite dangerous to the wearer unless they were part of a chain to impede mobility. But on the other hand, just one worn beneath the flowing robes of a woman would be well hidden from other's eyes, if necessary.'

John spoke up.

'Do you have any idea of the origin of these designs?'

'Unfortunately I do not. I feel that we must discover what these symbols and surface marks mean, before we can connect their place of origin.

Jubo joined in.

'I have also been interested in this subject and although I believe that the symbols are representations of cultural language, they could also suggest emblems or tokens used to make combinations which depict something other than what we see.'

Myra groaned. 'Jubo, that only confuses me more! What do you mean by combinations?'

'Well if you recall the ancient Egyptians wrote with small cuneiform symbols to make a sentence. This type of writing was also used in ancient Persia, Assyria and other remote civilizations. So as much as the artisans perpetuated the memory of certain designs, their knowledge in relation to nomadic lore has been diminished with each generation. I feel that these bracelets have to be read by an artisan with such knowledge.'

'I agree with you Jubo,' said James. Do you see anything that is similar to Ethiopian characters or letters?'

'I can't read anything in them but I know that many early invasions of Africa meant that displaced persons had to flee from their persecutors from Egypt to Morocco in Algeria, which is from one side of Africa to the other. So it is logical to assume that their jewelry would have moved with them, making the net wider, and our task more difficult. I can confirm that Ethiopian writing and language is not easily translated in any standard way into the Latin alphabet.'

Myra sighed.

'Where can we go from here?'

'Just to add to the confusion, Dan and I consider that Amharic is considered a sacred language and it may be possible that the symbols should be read in a phonetic fashion. For example the letter 'I' could actually mean 'eye.' The engraving is really a complex riddle.'

James made his thanks and departed, but Myra was not happy about the situation at all.

The answer came from Dan who found a clue in the museum archives in a book referring to a French archeological find in 1925. A chapter contained details about a fourth century woman called Tin Hinan whose tomb was opened to reveal the skeleton of a woman adorned with heavy gold and silver jewelry, some of it decorated with pearls. She wore a silver bracelet and there was another similar smaller silver bracelet and a gold ring placed on top of her body. These two bracelets were identical to the etchings shown to him by Mrs. Collins.

John recalled the conversation with the Tuareg, and now realized why he was not given the true picture about the bracelets. Myra was right. Abdel was only too happy to help in return for the two pieces, but it was perhaps from a sense of fierce loyalty for this special mysterious woman. If the tomb had already been opened and the remains removed to Algiers, why all the secrecy and why was there such a conspiracy to hide the message or its meaning? More questions to answer!

When John showed the book to James, there was a certain interest shown by him but he added a note of warning.

'Because of the similar designs on both, it must be remembered that it was a common practice for these engraved patterns to be copied throughout the generations, so even if you have some information which could link your bracelets to Tin Hinan, their value may be only from a provenance point of view.'

'I hear what you are saying James, but Dan has told me that he has a copy of the findings of that investigation after the tomb was found, so I think that Myra and I will read a little more about this remarkable woman.'

Armed with a large dossier they read about Tinan Hanan, but without any clues as to why the bracelet had 'skyline,' patterns. John read aloud.

'This is of some interest. Her tomb found in the Ahaggar mountain region of Algeria is surrounded by other tombs in the ancient capital of Abalessa.

She was believed to be a Muslim of the Braber tribe of Berbers who came from the Atlas Mountains in Morocco. She was also known as the Queen of the Tuaregs. Her grave was never plundered which showed how this African Amazon was held in the highest esteem by the Tuaregs.

Casting my mind back to a conversation which I had with Abdel, he admitted that the designs were distinctly Bedouin, and not unlike the Tuareg patterns, which should have told me something then. The Bedouins were like a rolling wave across Africa, and being nomads, it would not be beyond the realms of possibility that this design was perhaps from Ethiopia.' Myra stifled a yawn and said to John.

'Thank you for all that, but there is still more to learn about the bracelets which I think will take quite some time. That story is still waiting to be told.'

DAN'S DISCOVERY

John sat there reading about the nomadic races which were difficult to trace, because there was little left behind for archeologists to find. A known fact was that the Tuaregs did tell the stories of their people through their wonderful engravings on silver jewelry. This was their means of communicating their history as well as their culture. A culture and a history which they jealously guarded.

The next morning at breakfast, James was doing everything to grab the attention of his parents by throwing his cereal all over himself and his highchair. Jubo was hushing and fussing and cooing in his own language, but when he handed a rusk to James, peace prevailed.

'I think that I will write to Mohammed in Timbuktu and see how Norman is finding his new appointment, and also inform him that we have unearthed a little information concerning the origin of the two bracelets. Perhaps his contacts there may be able to decipher the wiggly lines, dots and dashes on these etchings,' John told his wife.

'Yes, why not,' agreed Myra.

'There is little more that we can do, except put this into the hands of language experts and hope that they can unlock it.'

Myra had not learned much about these objects but she had learned a great deal about being patient. This was going to take time.

John's current focus was on the political situation which only seemed to be worsening. Nelson Mandela had become a political activist with the banned African National Congress and although he was a lawyer, he was on trial for sabotage and attempting to overthrow the South African State. The court found that he had consistently advised their followers to adopt a peaceful course of action and avoid all violence. Mandela was given a suspended prison sentence. After reading the transcript of his trial, John was amazed at the simple truths espoused by Mandela, such as 'Africans want to be paid a living wage. Poverty and the breakdown of family have secondary effects. It is a struggle of the African people, inspired by their own suffering and their own experience. It is a struggle for the right to live. It is an ideal for which I am prepared to die.'

His thoughts were interrupted as Myra came in waving a letter.

'Jill and the family are coming here for a visit. They are hoping to make it for James's first birthday. Isn't that wonderful?' John was happy for Myra and the shared time with her sister as they would have much to discuss. On their arrival, this turned out to be a noisy and happy reunion. It took a little time for them to get know Jubo, but his sense of humour soon won them over.

Now that James was nearly walking, he used the furniture or one of his cousins to pull himself up and there was lots of giggles and a few 'ouches' if James decided to grab hold of Frances's hair. Her relatives were told by Frances that she thought that James sounded stuffy, so she was going to call him 'Jim from now on.

A letter arrived from Mohammed, but John delayed telling Myra about it.

'My dear colleague, it has been some time since we last shared each other's company, but I can still remember the pursuit of the manuscripts and your noble interest in them. The man sent by your Museum has turned out to be an apt pupil and a quick learner, and has been most useful to our cause. He has also suggested that in the near future, other Museums and Universities may join the race to protect and translate what is crumbling away. This seems a wonderful idea and is being discussed at length here. As to your comment about the bracelets, there has been a development which could shed some light on your quest. These details are not mine to divulge, but if you decide to make a journey here, my humble home will be at your convenience.

Sending my best wishes to your wife and son
I remain your friend
Mohammed.'

— CHAPTER FOUR —

Lost in Translation

Africa 1954

Myra was keen to show her sister and family the sights of Cape Town and that night at dinner asked John if could to take some time off from work.

'Strangely enough I have had the same idea, but this will depend on how long our relatives are staying with us.' John admitted.

'I would be pleased to show you this wonderful city and the surrounding areas. We both feel there is no hurry for you to leave.'

That night in the privacy of their bedroom, John showed Mohammed's letter to Myra. She was in two minds about it because she was torn between spending time with Jill and traveling to Timbuktu with her husband.

'I really don't have a choice. Even if I wanted to go with you, Jim is still too young to leave with Jubo, so it looks as if you alone will make that journey, but you can't guess just how much I would love to go too.'

John kissed her goodnight, and whispered.

'I have a very good idea my love, but you will hear all about it when I return. I haven't forgotten all that you went through, and I promise to make it up to you.'

John and Myra took delight in showing their Aussie relatives the sights and sounds of South Africa in the time allocated. John explained that he also had to make a trip to Timbuktu for a short time, which would allow Myra to spend time with Jill, Brian and family. He took the fastest route to Mali, where he was met by Mohammed who began with the customary tea ceremony at his home before the discussion began in earnest.

'When you informed me of the documented report of the French Army having found and entered the tomb of Tinan Hinan, it pinpointed the route for further investigation which has been relatively successful. To be perfectly frank, I had no idea of the origin or the inscriptions on those two bracelets. However it seems that the Tuareg Queen was found with an identical bracelet on her person. This of course must indicate that the design has been forged into a story which has been carried down through the ages by Tuareg artisans. What is engaging, is that one of your colleagues, namely Norman Banta has found amongst the countless manuscripts here, something which could be of interest to you.'

John was more than interested.

'If we can confirm the connection with Tinan Hinan, can we now can translate the inscriptions?'

Mohammed grinned.

'Firstly we need to know a little more about this Queen of the Legend, and her background history. You are well informed about the Bedouins and their lack of books and other such identifying written words, but to make it more difficult we know that Morocco had its own language before it came under the Islamic influence. Because this was developed long before the Christian era, the bracelet's symbols could have come from many other sources too.'

'I agree with your reasoning Mohammed but you have indicated that the old manuscripts have something to show me so perhaps we can talk about that.'

'Yes John, the knowledge made available to me is not conclusive evidence and is for your eyes only.'

'Very well, please tell me what you have found out.'

Mohammed chose his words carefully because he did not want to insult his colleague by informing him that this sharing of information might be frowned upon in some circles.

'Part of this story is already known by the Western world, as it was reported that the tomb of

Tinan Hinan contained many silver and gold items. What was not reported was the fact that there were some Roman coins issued between 308 and 324 A.D also included in her grave. This confirmed the carbon dating of her wooden litter as being made in the 4th or 5th century A.D. There was also pottery and other tomb furniture, which has given us a better picture of her.'

'What does this tell us about her?' asked John.

'Any detail is important when doing this kind of research, and because she was in possession of some Roman coins, it opens a completely different theory about her life. You will recall that there was a rumour told by the Tuaregs that a lost Roman Legion came to live with them, which is seen today in their eye colour and chiseled features. These coins could be proof of that connection. We will visit our local Museum where a friend will tell us something about all this, but anything that you hear will have to remain confidential for reasons which will be explained to you there.'

At the museum Norman Banta joined them for the tea ceremony. He was happy to meet again with John and received praise and appreciation for his part in this new discovery. The senior Curator took control of the proceedings which he conducted in a solemn tone.

'Mr. Collins as you already know, we live in a world of shifting ideals, religions, borders and in the case here, encroaching sand which threatens to swallow up our city and our precious threads of history and learning. We have been happy to have your colleague Mr.Banta here to assist in the deciphering of a past history found amongst our manuscripts. In the case of Tinan Hinan, it is said that she built a 'Skyscraper City' amongst the Ahaggar Mountains in Algeria, after she had left the Atlas Mountains in Morocco. This may explain the unusual patterns found on the bracelet etchings, but in my opinion they serve no purpose except to define the region where she ruled. What is really important is this. She was credited as being the first leader to unite the Tuareg world and to establish a kingdom, which was quite an achievement because the Tuaregs as you know were nomads and to this day still prefer the desert to city dwelling.

Now as to the symbols: After consulting with my fellows here at the Museum, we believe that the engravings hold a secret, some of which we have uncovered. There is no treasure nor is there any reference to one, but the words which have been revealed are of the highest human aspirations which we all strive to attain. These are 'Peace, Freedom and Hope.'

The other words or symbols seem to be of a personal nature, which we can only guess at, but I would now like to refer to the manuscript.'

LOST IN TRANSLATION

John remembered his first experience with the crumbling books and carefully watched as an old book which was covered with a lightweight cloth, was handled as if it was a piece of delicate gossamer. The reader explained that the paper was so brittle that it could snap at any moment and so the cloth was used to prevent any further loss of moisture. The pages seemed to consist of loose folios which did not adhere to any spine, but were secured by flaps which wrapped around the entire volume, supporting the contents.

'When Mohammed first approached me with your enquiries about the Tuareg Queen, I was not in favour to disclose anything more about her. The original discovery of her tomb seemed to be enough for the western world to digest, and it seemed disloyal to take it any further. However Mohammed had informed me of your efforts in sending Norman Banta here through a scholarship to help us with our seemingly endless task of restoration and translation of this treasure house of knowledge. It is because of Mohammed's faith in you, and your obvious practical assistance, that I will read to you from a book which has been here for centuries. However you know that there is little hope that anything from the 4th or 5th century could have survived until today, except perhaps for those engravings on the bracelets. What I am about to reveal is a letter supposedly written by one of her descendants and passed down through the line of female ancestors.'

"I have arisen from my meditation chamber, but still the pain grips my heart, and nothing can assuage my grief. My dearest maidservant lies dead. She meant more to me than I could ever show. Her passing was so cruel. For many years she was my faithful friend and companion, her wisdom and guidance were always eagerly sought by me. The day she died was like no other. Even though we were accompanied by a Centurion, a lone Cheetah found us walking in the mountains and would have killed me.

Takamat, you gave up your life to save mine. When you are buried in a tomb, it shall be close to the one which I have chosen for myself. I shall keep your small silver bracelet from your wrist and it will serve as a reminder of our days together.'

John was silent, thinking of how Myra would have loved to hear this wonderful human story about a woman who had lived so long ago. She had mourned for a friend so intimately, and shown great appreciation to someone who had been her mentor and her closest friend. As a Queen, she had cherished harmony and freedom. At the same time she had been responsible for the unity of the wandering tribes of the Sahara. Her wisdom had embraced empathy, hope and peace and was certainly a blueprint for the future. The two bracelets were obvious copies from the time of Tinan Hinan, and part of a story which would be fully revealed someday. He also realised why these details were to be kept hidden. When the tomb had been entered, it would have been seen as a violation in the eyes of her people, but also if what he had just heard became common knowledge it wouldn't be long before a search was made for Takamat.

'I thank you sincerely for this wonderful insight which you have shown me. The disclosure of this story and how it came to be kept here is perhaps a story in itself, but you have my word it will remain safely with me.'

John stood, shook hands with the Curator and began to leave. He stopped to talk with Mohammed.

'There are some things which we will never know but I am pleased to have learned something about the provenance surrounding the bracelets.

One thing which I must do before I go is to have a look at the Ethiopian display. Myra and I found an interesting object there and I would like to know something more about it.'

When he pointed it out to his friend, Mohammed began to laugh. 'An Ear Spoon: Those things can be found any day in the market place. As you rightly said, they are Ethiopian, but this design has been copied and adapted by the people who live here. The sand is a common enemy and creeps into many places where it is not wanted, so the ear spoon is a common and useful tool. We will find you one before you return home.'

'Thanks. In that case we will make it three. One for Myra, one for Jubo who originally came from Ethiopia, and one for his son Dan who was responsible for finding the information about Tinan Hinan. My wife has had a very interesting connection to Silver Spoons and this one will be no exception.'

John looked around to say goodbye to Norman Banta who was nowhere to be seen. The reason for this was that Norman was not entirely happy with what had happened here today. There was more to the story told by the Curator, but it wasn't his place to correct or enquire as to why so much had been omitted.

As the two men left, the Curator carefully closed the book. He had read only what he deemed prudent to serve the purpose.

There was a much richer and more mysterious tale behind the origins of the bracelets, but it had to remain concealed. Perhaps John Collins would return at another time. The truth had been hidden for centuries: the translations would survive a little longer.

A.E. Stewart

This author began telling stories at the age of six in a Sydney boarding school. Once lights were out, tall tales were in. 'Ghost stories' were the most popular but it was the repetition of speaking and composing which produced words at a speed far quicker than anyone could write them down that started the treadmill. Such a place became the nursery where a vivid imagination was born.

A.E. lived in England for some time prior to the Queen's Coronation, where a wealth of experience with the 'Cockney' way of life and the different accents of the London population was gained.

The series of 'The Silver Thieves' was born from a younger brother's inspiration. His love of Silver and the borrowed 'Sterling Silver and their Hallmarks' book became the catalyst for this writer's literary intentions.

If you enjoyed this book, please leave a review on Amazon.

Contact A.E. ....jacana3@bigpond.com

The Queen's Coronation Spoon is stolen, leaving Myra to avert a national disaster.

Then in 1952 she comes into possession of a spoon stolen right from under the nose of Captain Cook himself, straight off the Endeavour in 1770.

Shrewd buyers circle, but a stubborn Myra obsessed with discovering the origin of Cook's spoon, hangs on through insurmountable challenges.

Excitement turns to disaster for Myra during the Queen's Coronation but the discovery of a cache of silver lifts her spirits; until religious fanatics ruin her honeymoon in Timbuktu.

A race against time to save the crumbling manuscripts of Timbuktu demand John's serious attention, but Myra's needs take priority as her life hangs in the balance.

The translation of the origin and the engraved message of the silver bracelets are revealed to John, but has he heard the whole story?

In the fourth century A.D. a young woman unites the nomadic Tuareg tribes of the Saharan Desert region.

Loved and known as the "Mother of us all," she is called Queen Tinan Hinan.

She commissions two silver bracelets, the engravings forming a map to the hiding place of a vast treasure.

But this connection to an ancient culture prevents anyone from unlocking the secret.